BONKERS

About Beetroot

written by
Cath Jones

illustrated by
Chris Jevons

It was another quiet day at Sunset Safari Park.

"Good evening Penguin!" called Zebra.

But Penguin scowled.

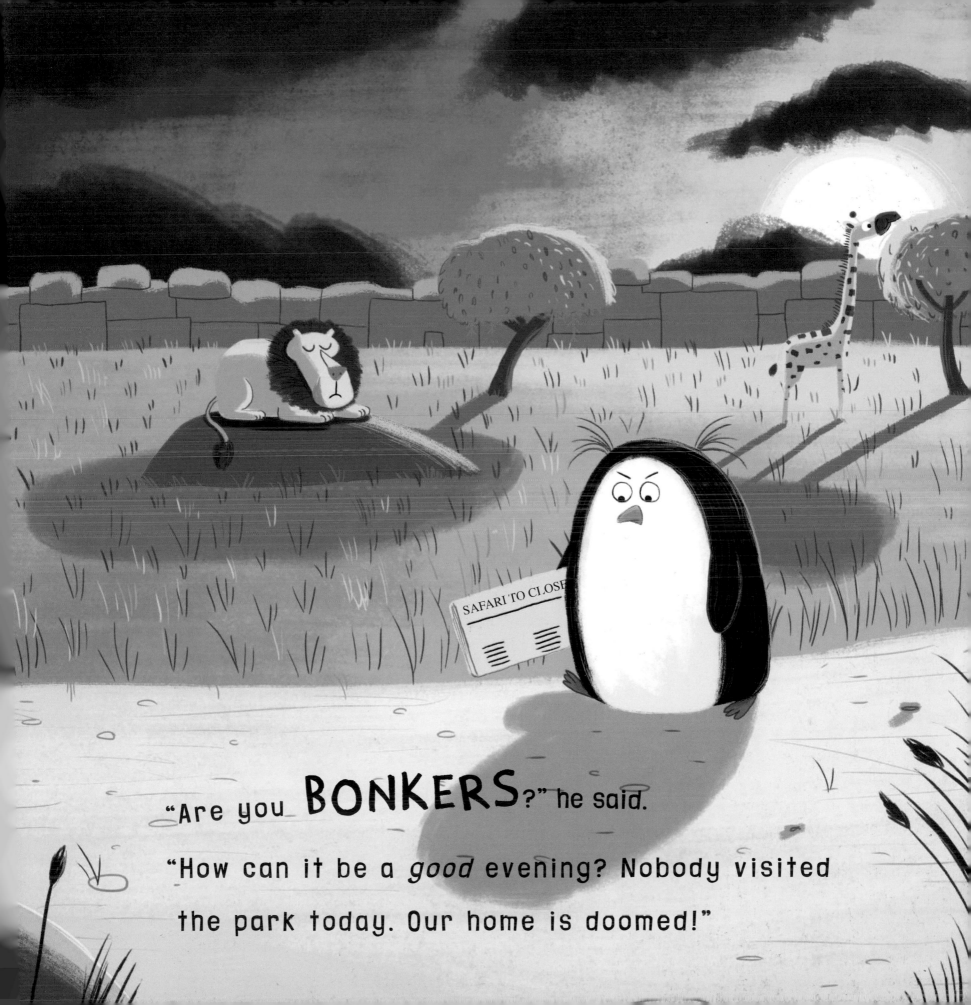

"Are you BONKERS?" he said.

"How can it be a *good* evening? Nobody visited the park today. Our home is doomed!"

Zebra called a meeting.

"We have to find more visitors," he said,

"We need to save our park."

"You're wasting your time," Penguin said.

"Nobody comes because we're boring."

But Zebra tried anyway.

The animals hunted for the missing visitors.

Suddenly, Zebra let out a yell...

"Beetroot?" Penguin asked.

Zebra nodded. "People are crazy about beetroot. We must grow the biggest beetroot in the world."

"BONKERS!" said Penguin. "No one will visit a BEETROOT safari park."

But Zebra tried anyway.

He made a list of everything they would need.

So the
animals built
a **mighty** manure
mountain.

"STOP!" shouted Penguin.
"That's a **BONKERS** manure heap."

The animals
planted the seeds.

They watered.

The seeds began to grow.

One plant grew bigger

than the rest...

The beetroot **grew** and **grew**...

BONKERS
BEETROOT!

RUMBLE
SQUELCH
RUSTLE
This vegetable is out of control, I have to stop it!

It grew **BIGGER** and **BIGGER**.

Soon there was no room for visitors!

MONSTER BEETROOT
TAKES OVER PARK

Zebra began to **EAT** the giant beetroot.

"Are you **BONKERS**?" said Penguin.
"You can't eat all that."

But Zebra tried anyway.

WWWOOOOOO,"

moaned Zebra.

"HELP!" cried the animals, "Zebra is ill."
"Zebra's not ill," said Penguin. "But he's...

...turned **PURPLE!**"

Thousands of visitors arrived to see the only purple zebra in the world!

Sunset Park

"Hooray for Zebra!" cheered the animals.

"He's saved our home."

FRESH
BEETROOT

And Penguin said...

THE END.

Bonkers About Beetroot

An original concept by author Cath Jones

© Cath Jones

Illustrated by Chris Jevons

MAVERICK ARTS PUBLISHING LTD

Studio 3A, City Business Centre, 6 Brighton Road, Horsham, West Sussex, RH13 5BB

© Maverick Arts Publishing Limited   +44 (0)1403 256941

Published September 2017

A CIP catalogue record for this book is available at the British Library.

ISBN 978-1-84886-281-4

Maverick
arts publishing

www.maverickbooks.co.uk

PURPLE ZEBRA
SAVES SAFARI PARK